I0607115

New York Chamber of Commerce

Tribute of the Chamber of Commerce

of the State of New-York to the memory of General Wm. T. Sherman.

February 17, 1891

New York Chamber of Commerce

Tribute of the Chamber of Commerce
of the State of New-York to the memory of General Wm. T. Sherman. February 17, 1891

ISBN/EAN: 9783337093976

Printed in Europe, USA, Canada, Australia, Japan

Cover: Foto ©Andreas Hilbeck / pixelio.de

More available books at **www.hansebooks.com**

TRIBUTE

OF THE

CHAMBER OF COMMERCE

OF THE

STATE OF NEW-YORK

TO THE MEMORY OF

GENERAL WM. T. SHERMAN.

FEBRUARY 17, 1891.

———————

NEW-YORK:

PRESS OF THE CHAMBER OF COMMERCE.

—

1891.

TRIBUTE

TO THE MEMORY OF

GENERAL WM. T. SHERMAN.

To afford the merchants and business men of New-York an opportunity to express, in a public manner, their regard for the memory of General SHERMAN, their sympathy for his bereaved family, and their sense of the loss sustained by the nation of a great soldier, patriot and statesman, a special meeting of the Chamber of Commerce was held Tuesday, February 17th, 1891.

Mr. CHARLES S. SMITH, President of the Chamber, presided, and said:

GENTLEMEN: General SHERMAN, the last of the great leaders in our late war, has followed LINCOLN and FARRAGUT, SEWARD and CHASE, GRANT, SHERIDAN and PORTER to the tomb.

In the death of SHERMAN this Chamber has not
only lost its most conspicuous honorary member,
but a friend endeared to us by intimate association,
and to whom we are indebted for many kind and
considerate acts. It is impossible to appreciate the
grandeur of a great mountain peak when standing
near its base. And so with the life of a great man.
The perspective of time and distance is necessary to
determine the exact place which the final judgment
of posterity will assign to him. It is absolutely cer-
tain that history will write the name of WILLIAM
TECUMSEH SHERMAN conspicuously upon the page
devoted to those who founded and saved the
Republic ; and his memory will be cherished in the
hearts of the people as long as patriotic service,
unswerving integrity and lovable qualities are ap-
preciated among men.

RESOLUTIONS.

Mr. J. EDWARD SIMMONS offered the following
preamble and resolutions, and moved their adoption :

Whereas, The members of the Chamber of Commerce but a short time since were called to assemble
in the presence of a severe national bereavement to
pay their tribute of respect to the character and

noble labors of a distinguished civilian and statesman, having under his care the fiduciary interests of
the Republic ; and

Whereas, To-day, by the dispensation of an all-
wise Providence, we meet to pay our tribute of
affectionate regard to the memory of a great soldier
whose splendid services in the long struggle for the
preservation of the Union were as brilliant as they
were successful, and whose achievements illustrated
the greatness of a soldier who in conquest knew no
hate, and in whose magnanimity there was no
revenge ; therefore,

Resolved, That the Chamber of Commerce of the
State of New-York hereby places on record its
unanimous sentiment of profound sorrow because of
the irreparable bereavement the nation has sustained
in the death of our distinguished soldier citizen,
General WILLIAM TECUMSEH SHERMAN.

Resolved, That by the death of General SHERMAN
the world has lost one of its greatest military heroes.
Pure in heart, of spotless integrity, cool and undis-
mayed in danger, he not only won honor and renown
from the soldiers of his command, but he invariably
inspired them with confidence, friendship and affection. He was the soldier of Justice, Right and

Truth, and he has passed from our midst as a brilliant star pales and vanishes from the morning sky.

Resolved, That the results achieved by the late war were largely due to the consummate skill, adroit strategy and matchless generalship of WILLIAM TECUMSEH SHERMAN, and that the people of this Republic are indebted to him for his eminent services in securing to them the inestimable blessings of a united and prosperous country.

Resolved, That as a public spirited citizen he proved himself to be a capable man of affairs, with a deep interest in many of our local institutions. As an honorary member he has presided over the deliberations of this Chamber, and his genial presence was seldom missed at our annual banquets. Socially he was the peer of those with whom companionship had a charm, and illustrated in his intercourse all the qualities of a nobleman in the amenities of life. His home was a haven of repose, and love and gentleness were the angels that ministered at his fireside.

Resolved, That the Chamber of Commerce hereby tenders to the family of General SHERMAN the expression of sincere sympathy in the hour of their bereavement.

ADDRESS BY THE HON. CARL SCHURZ.

GENTLEMEN : The adoption by the Chamber of
Commerce of these resolutions which I have the
honor to second, is no mere perfunctory proceeding.
We have been called here by a genuine impulse of
the heart. To us General SHERMAN was not a great
man like other great men, honored and revered at a
distance. We had the proud and happy privilege
of calling him one of us. Only a few months ago,
at the annual meeting of this Chamber, we saw the
familiar face of our honorary member on this plat-
form by the side of our President. Only a few
weeks ago he sat at our banquet table, as he had
often before, in the happiest mood of conviviality,
and contributed to the enjoyment of the night with
his always unassuming and always charming speech.
And as he moved among us without the slightest
pomp of self-conscious historic dignity, only with
the warm and simple geniality of his nature, it
would cost us sometimes an effort of the memory to
recollect that he was the renowned captain who had
marshaled mighty armies victoriously on many a
battlefield, and whose name stood, and will for ever
stand, in the very foremost rank of the saviours of
this Republic, and of the great soldiers of the
world's history. Indeed, no American could have

forgotten this for a moment; but the affection of those who were so happy as to come near to him, would sometimes struggle to outrun their veneration and gratitude.

Death has at last conquered the hero of so many campaigns; our cities and towns and villages are decked with flags at half-mast; the muffled drum and the funereal cannon-boom will resound over the land as his dead body passes to the final resting place; and the American people stand mournfully gazing into the void left by the sudden disappearance of the last of the greatest men brought forth by our war of regeneration,—and this last also finally become, save ABRAHAM LINCOLN alone, the most widely beloved. He is gone; but as we of the present generation remember it, history will tell all coming centuries the romantic story of the famous " March to the Sea,"—how, in the dark days of 1864, SHERMAN, having worked his bloody way to Atlanta, then cast off all his lines of supply and communication, and, like a bold diver into the dark unknown, seemed to vanish with all his hosts from the eyes of the world, until his triumphant reappearance on the shores of the ocean proclaimed to the anxiously expecting millions, that now the final victory was no longer doubtful, and that the Republic would surely be saved.

Nor will history fail to record that this great

general was, as a victorious soldier, a model of
republican citizenship. When he had done his
illustrious deeds, he rose step by step to the highest
rank in the army, and then, grown old, he retired.
The Republic made provision for him in modest
republican style. He was satisfied. He asked for
no higher reward. Although the splendor of his
achievements, and the personal affection for him,
which every one of his soldiers carried home, made
him the most popular American of his day, and
although the most glittering prizes were not seldom
held up before his eyes, he remained untroubled by
ulterior ambition. No thought that the Republic
owed him more ever darkened his mind. No man
could have spoken to him of the "ingratitude of
Republics," without meeting from him a stern
rebuke. And so, content with the consciousness of
a great duty nobly done, he was happy in the love
of his fellow citizens.

Indeed, he may truly be said to have been in his old
age, not only the most beloved, but also the happiest
of Americans. Many years he lived in the midst of
posterity. His task was finished, and this he wisely
understood. His deeds had been passed upon by
the judgment of history, and irrevocably registered
among the glories of his country and his age. His
generous heart envied no one, and wished every
one well; and ill-will had long ceased to pursue him.

Beyond cavil his fame was secure, and he enjoyed it as that which he had honestly earned, with a genuine and ever fresh delight, openly avowed by the charming frankness of his nature. He dearly loved to be esteemed and cherished by his fellow-men, and what he valued most, his waning years brought him in ever increasing abundance. Thus he was in truth a most happy man, and his days went down like an evening sun in a cloudless autumn sky. And when now the American people, with that peculiar tenderness of affection which they have long borne him, lay him in his grave, the happy ending of his great life may soothe the pang of bereavement they feel in their hearts at the loss of the old hero who was so dear to them, and of whom they were and always will be so proud. His memory will ever be bright to us all; his truest monument will be the greatness of the Republic he served so well ; and his fame will never cease to be prized by a grateful country, as one of its most precious possessions.

ADDRESS BY GENERAL HORACE PORTER.

MR. PRESIDENT AND GENTLEMEN : I take a
pleasure, mingled with inexpressible grief, in rising
to second the very appropriate resolutions submitted
in honor of the memory of the last of our pre-eminent
military chieftains. While we all share in the
general grief of the nation, I know that there are
many members of this body upon whom the blow
falls individually—those who, like myself, have
been associated upon terms of intimacy with General
SHERMAN, both in war and in peace, and to whom
this news come home with a sorrow which is akin to
the grief of a personal bereavement.

By no act of ours can we expect to add one more
laurel to his brow. The world has already heaped
upon him all its honors. The nation raised him to
the highest military rank ; Congress tendered him
votes of thanks ; our leading universities vied with
each other in conferring upon him their highest
degrees ; at home and abroad, clubs and societies
made him an honorary member; innumerable medals
have been struck in his honor. We cannot expect
to add to his earthly glory. We can only gather
together and respectfully testify our esteem for the
soldier, our affection for the man.

While General SHERMAN was a person of marvel-

lous versatility of talent, while he was a many-sided
man, while he possessed rare qualities and had enjoyed a varied experience in most of the useful walks
of life, yet his great fame will always rest upon his
merits as a soldier. With him the chief character-
istics of the soldier seemed unborn. In his very
walk, in his very look, there was something which
always spoke of the typical soldier ; with his
closely-knit brows, his deep, penetrating, restless
eyes, his aquiline nose, there was something in his
look which savored of the piercing glance of the
eagle. In war he was bold in conception, fixed in
purpose, and untiring in effort. He was singularly
self-reliant, always demonstrated by his acts, that
"much danger makes great hearts most resolute."
He possessed an intuitive knowledge of topography.
He seemed to combine in his own person the patience
of a FABIUS with the restlessness of a HOTSPUR. He
was fertile in expedients, and quick to adapt the
means at hand to the accomplishment of an end.
He enjoyed a personal reputation unsullied, of un-
impeachable integrity. He had a physique which
enabled him to endure all the hardships incident to
the most active campaign. It was no wonder that
the world placed him in the first rank of the earth's
great captains.

Students of military history, both at home and
abroad, have studied his campaigns and made them

their models. They have ranked his work on a
level with that of the great masters of military
science.

The popular mind will always be fond of picturing
him as a chieftain whose field of military operations
covered nearly half a continent; as a commander
whose orders always spoke with the true bluntness
of the soldier, as a leader who had penetrated ever-
glades and bayous, who had fought from valleys'
depths to mountain heights, and marched from
inland rivers to the sea.

He possessed one conspicuous characteristic which
I am sure all have noticed, and that was that in all
his writings, in all his speeches, he always uttered
the loftiest sentiments of patriotism. In his ad-
dresses to the old and young, he never failed to
inculcate in their minds the principle that the
highest type of virtue in the citizen or the soldier
is a love of country. Who can ever forget the
last time we met him in this very Chamber, when
he honored us by coming here and delivering that
memorable address of welcome to the Pan-American
Congress, an address so full of historical incidents,
so replete with the loftiest sentiments of patriotism,
so expressive of his pride in the progress of the
country, and his unalterable faith in its great
future. So marvellous was that address, that when
he ceased to speak a painful sense of stillness

seemed to fall upon the ear, and the representatives
of all the Americas sat spellbound under the charm.

His death has caused a gap in this community
which time and men can never fill. We thought we
had a right to expect, from the elasticity of his step,
from the activity of his life, from the possession of all
his marvellous faculties, that we might have him here
among us and enjoy his companionship for years to
come ; but Providence ordered it otherwise, and we
can only bow to the decree. We have said our last
farewell to the illustrious soldier, the silver cord has
been loosed, the golden bowl has been broken, and
his spirit has winged its flight from earth ; we shall
not meet the great leader again until he stands
forth to answer to his name at roll call on the morning of the last great *reveille.* The laurel on his brow
is now intertwined with the cypress, the flag he so
often upheld has dropped to half-mast, the echo of
his guns has given place to the tolling of cathedral
bells, and America finds herself once more standing
within the shadow of a profound grief. There is
some consolation, some compensation in his death—
it is the consciousness that the country and the
world are better for his having lived therein ; that
he has handed down to posterity the richest legacy
which man can leave to man—the memory of a good
name—the inheritance of a great example.

ADDRESS BY THE HON. ABRAM S. HEWITT.

MR. PRESIDENT : I came here prepared to listen,
not to speak, and after the singularly eloquent and
just tributes which have been made to the memory
of our departed hero, I feel reluctant to trench upon
ground which has been covered by the resolutions
and the graceful remarks of the President, Mr.
SCHURZ and General PORTER. But it occurs to me
that I may with propriety refer to some points in
the career of General SHERMAN which shed a new
light upon his character and lustre upon his fame.
These incidents are known only to me, and it is not
inappropriate to make them known to others. We
all remember the agitation of the country at the
time when the Electoral Commission was passing in
1877, upon the disputed succession to the Presidency.
General SHERMAN was then at the head of the army.
The term of President GRANT was coming to a
close ; the electoral count had not been finished, and
there was great apprehension on the part of patriotic
men that Congress might break up without deciding
who had been elected President. The horrors of the
Civil War from which we had emerged seemed about
to be renewed.

Profoundly impressed with the dangers of the
situation, it occurred to me that I ought to have a

consultation with General SHERMAN, and to ask him
what would be his course as commanding officer of
the army of the United States in case the count
should not be completed. We had an interview in
which I explained the situation and discussed the
dangers which might follow. He coincided with
me as to the peril before us, when I asked him what
his course would be in case the count should not be
finished, and the services of the army might be re-
quired to preserve public order. I told him that
suggestions had been made that President GRANT,
under the circumstances, ought to hold over in
order to prevent the chaos which would ensue from
a vacancy in the office of President. I asked General
SHERMAN whether, under such circumstances, he
would obey the orders of President GRANT. He
replied :

"Mr. HEWITT, I have sworn to obey the Constitution of the United States, and I will perform my
duty. The term of President GRANT ends at twelve
o'clock on the 4th of March. He will then be in no
position to give orders to me, and I shall receive no
orders from him, but I will take care that the
dangers of anarchy shall not be experienced by the
country. The people have elected a President, and
a competent authority will be found to declare who
is elected, and I shall obey the orders of the one who

shall be declared to be President of the United States."

I replied, "General SHERMAN, the difficulty is that the two Houses may disagree, and there may be no completion of the count. What would you then do?"

He said, "I trust that the responsibility will not be placed upon me, but if it shall happen that I must elect between the two undoubted candidates for the office, and Congress shall break up without declaring the result in consequence of the failure of the House to do its duty, I shall be constrained to recognize the mandate of the Senate of the United States as decisive of the question."

I said to him, "General, there is no precedent for such a course, and the Senate will not have the right to decide the question."

To this he replied : "It must be decided by somebody; and in the presence of a danger which involves the safety of the Union and the peace and order of the country, the General of the army would be compelled to recognize the underlying principle that the safety of the people is the supreme law."

I replied : "General, I do not see that you can take any other course, because it would be a fatal precedent if the President should hold over, and it was mainly to get your opinion upon that point that I have sought this interview."

Of course, I knew what his decision meant, and that the candidate, whose election I had advocated, would not be recognized by him as President. I knew also that the country would be saved from civil war. It was the knowledge of this fact that contributed very largely to the completion of the count. Certainly, great gratitude is due to General SHERMAN for his military services, but I think we will all recognize now that his action in a moment of public peril preserved the stability of the country, and entitles him to the highest credit for firmness and patriotism. We not only owe to him the completion of the civil war, and the regeneration of the Republic, but he is entitled to our gratitude for having preserved us from untold calamities which would have followed a conflict between political parties, dividing every family and household in the land.

One other fact, and I am done. When General SHERMAN was about to be retired from the office of General, in consequence of having reached the statutory limitation, which in the army was 62 years, there was a very general desire on the part of the public, concurred in by the members of Congress, to repeal the limitation of the statute in his case, as it had been made inoperative in the case of Admiral PORTER. As I was Chairman of the Sub-Committee in charge of the Army Appropriation Bill, I was

asked to see General SHERMAN, and ascertain whether an amendment to the bill, removing the statutory limitation in his case, would be acceptable. His reply was instantaneous :

"No; I am a soldier and a citizen. I always obey the law ; I do not desire to have a change in my favor, as it expresses the judgment of the people in regard to the duration of military service. Besides, there are other officers who have rights in the premises. If I remain here, others will be deprived of promotion. No ; I will not accept any lengthening of my term of service ; but when the time arrives for me to retire, I will go into the ranks of private life and perform my duties as a citizen, leaving to others the exercise of military power which belongs to this office."

I know of nothing more beautiful in the character of any man who has ever come under my notice than the inherent patriotism which characterized every element of General SHERMAN's character. I know of nothing more admirable than the unselfish way in which he was ready to lay down rank and power on the altar of Justice. He has set an example to us, and to the generations who are to come after us, the value of which cannot be estimated. If the time should ever come when selfish ambition should lead towards a military despotism, the example of General SHERMAN will, I am sure, save us from im-

pending calamity, and will encourage the people to preserve their Government even at the cost of fortune and life.

ADDRESS BY MR. WILLIAM E. DODGE.

MR. PRESIDENT AND GENTLEMEN OF THE CHAM-
BER : Some of us who are here remember, with
deep emotion, those last days of the war, and how
the tension under which we had been held for so many
years was loosened when news came of the surrender
of LEE. We remember how, by a common impulse,
great masses of the people gathered in Wall Street,
in Pearl Street and in William Street, and from a
hundred thousand throats went up that glad dox-
logy of thanksgiving to GOD.

LINCOLN and GRANT and SHERMAN we had loved
and trusted before. Then they were enshrined in
our hearts. Years have come and gone—years of
peace and prosperity and marvellous advance ; but
the lustre of these great names has never grown
dim, and we have loved them more and honored
them more sincerely as those years went by.

LINCOLN'S tragic death, GRANT'S political life and
his long, lingering illness, touching our hearts, kept
those two great souls from the enjoyment and honor
which would have come to them if they had lived
as SHERMAN did.

As has been so well said to-day, SHERMAN really
lived in posterity. His life has been most unique.

After a magnificent preparation for work—after a

great life of heroic courage and grand service for the
country he loved so much, he came to the duties of
a simple citizen with a heartiness and sincerity and
fullness of life that made him loved by everybody.

There has been something very delightful about
the life of General SHERMAN in New-York. Even
during this last winter, wherever he has been he has
met with a love and admiration which have been
wonderful. Into whatever company he came he was
easily first. "Where he sat was the head of the
table." And, although I think he had but little
vanity or egotism, he must certainly have enjoyed
the admiration of the people about him just as a
father loves the glad sparkle in the eyes of his children when he comes to them.

Some great men need no eulogy. They have impressed themselves so fully upon the age that no
words will add to the impression they have left.
The most eloquent words that can be spoken of such
men are but weak. In the full heart of every patriotic man here, tender and grateful thoughts, moving
more rapidly than the words of any speaker, will be
to each one a better eulogy of the life of such a man
as SHERMAN.

I think that as merchants there is a peculiar fitness
in our gathering to express our love and honor for
the memory of this great man.

During the war no class of people in this country

did more loyal service than the merchants of this city. They gave freely of their money and their time; many gave themselves or their children. They had everything at stake.

When SHERMAN swung off towards the sea, with those splendid soldiers, HOWARD and SLOCUM, and was lost to sight, what a tension of feeling there was through all this city. We knew it was the crisis of the war, and our hearts bounded with hope and gladness when the news came that he had reached the sea, and that the beginning of the end had come.

So much has been said, and said so well, as to the character of this grand old man, that I shall say nothing more, but I hope I shall be pardoned for a single word as to the lesson these great lives teach us. Their personal presence has gone. There is nothing now but the happy memory of grand and heroic service.

But we must remember that peace has duties as great, and dangers as real, as war. There is an opportunity for full and heroic lives to be lived in these times, and if these great souls could come back to life, I know there is nothing would fill their hearts with such delight as to feel that some of the robustness of manhood, and vigor in action, they showed in war, were being shown by us in our daily lives and duties here.

Republics have not gone down in wars. They have gone down from the enervation that came with luxury and self-indulgence, and all the dangers that follow wealth and prosperity.

We, as merchants, as men of affairs, who have a stake here, must take our stand valiantly, and try to preserve the heritage they have left us.

The other night I had the privilege of attending a most impressive gathering. The great hall of Cooper Institute was filled to overflowing, and almost as many on the outside, of those who had been the recipients of the bounty and the wise and thoughtful kindness of our dear friend, the late Mr. PETER COOPER.

I was touched by a remark made by a distinguished speaker, who had been chosen when a pupil of the school to make an address to Mr. COOPER on one of his birthdays. He said Mr. COOPER gave them good advice in reply, and then added, "Young men, my object in business has been to make as much money as I could honestly and honorably, but my object in life has been to do good to those who are about me."

If such a great impulse can come into our lives, drawing us away from the dangers that come in these days of prosperity and peace, we can establish our manhood and do our duty with something of the same magnificent courage shown by those great souls who have left us.

The President submitted the following letter from General THOMAS HILLHOUSE, who was unable to attend the meeting :

NEW-YORK, *February* 17, 1891.

DEAR SIR : I regret that circumstances will prevent me from attending the meeting of the Chamber of Commerce to-day, but I do most sincerely approve the object and purpose for which it is called.

One by one the great commanders of the Civil War disappear from the theatre of their memorable achievements. GRANT, SHERIDAN, THOMAS, MEADE, and now SHERMAN. They have done their work ; they have fought their last battles ; and it only remains for history to record their deeds, and to give them their proper rank amongst the great commanders of the world.

These are not words of mere adulation. If sectional animosities are forgotten ; if a race has been set free ; if the Union, one and indivisible, still reflects its benignant light throughout the world ; if "government of the people, by the people and for the people has not perished from the earth," it is due in no small measure to the men who so successfully led the armies of the Union to final victory. They were the trusted lieutenants of the great President in his struggle to maintain the integrity of this Government. They took up their work with faith in them-

selves, faith in the cause, and faith in the magnificent
armies they commanded, and they accomplished it.

And now SHERMAN. He too has followed his
comrades in arms ; he too has joined "the innumerable host that moves to the pale realms of shade ;"
but he was spared to see the end of the contest in
which he bore so conspicuous a part. The army
confided to him, he directed with consummate skill
to a definite purpose, and that purpose had been
accomplished. The Confederacy had been rent in
twain ; its heart had been pierced. Not to him
had his Commander-in-Chief to address the de-
spairing cry of the Roman Emperor, "VARUS,
restore me my legions." There they were, singed
with the fire, and begrimed with the smoke of
battle on those ever memorable days of May, 1865,
when the armies of the Union marched through
the Capital, the very embodiment of the power
of the people put forth in defence of their Constitution and Government. No man in the vast assem-
bly that witnessed the pageant doubted that the
spirit of disunion had been crushed. No doubter,
but believed in the right and the power of the Government to defend its existence by a coercion of
arms, when a coercion of laws had failed. The right
and the power had received their complete and final
vindication.

Of SHERMAN, as one of our great commanders,

this is not the time nor place to speak at length. The history of the vast military operations of our civil war, that is to be the final authority, will not appear until the passions, the prejudices and the preferences of the present generation shall have passed into oblivion. Then some future JOMINI, out of the abundant materials at hand, will weave a narrative of those operations, comprehensive in its scope, and just in its criticisms of men and measures. Is it hazardous to predict, that the " March to the Sea " will be regarded as one of the most brilliant and decisive of all the campaigns of the war, and the commander, who so successfully conceived and executed it, one of the greatest masters of military science ?

It was after the evacuation of Atlanta that SHER-MAN, as he tells us in his Memoirs, decided to cut loose from his base and lead his victorious armies to the sea—an inspiration of genius, like his views on the conduct of the war at an earlier period, regarded with doubt and anxiety in official circles, only to be triumphantly vindicated by its complete success. "None of us went further than to acquiesce," was the frank admission of the President. The obstacles to be encountered, and the means at hand to overcome them, had been measured with almost scientific exactness, and when the campaign had been finished by the fall of Savannah and the

surrender at Greensboro, there was no dissent from
the conclusion, that it had been more fruitful in
grand results than any of the events of the war, save
only the almost cotemporaneous surrender at Ap-
pomattox, and the disintegration of the Confederate
Government.

But the military fame of SHERMAN will not rest
wholly on his march to the sea. To the diligent
student, the operations that preceded it are full of
interest and instruction. From Dalton to the cross-
ing of the Chattahoochee he was confronted by as
consummate a master of defensive warfare as either
side had produced. Here on a field admirably
adapted to the most brilliant display of strategy and
tactical skill, these great leaders contended for victory; and when SHERMAN entered Atlanta, his ob-
jective point, he had already earned his place in the
front rank of our Commanders.

Of SHERMAN, the patriotic citizen, free from all
political ambition, intent only on employing his
great talents for the public good, the verdict of the
people has long since gone forth, and it is voiced to-
day in the public expressions of sorrow which the
announcement of his death has called out throughout the land. Such a verdict was doubtless more
precious in his eyes than all the distinctions of
office, or all the attractions of wealth. His civic
virtues will not pale even before the splendor of his

military renown. His loyalty was intense. It pervaded his whole being. It gave him strength and patience to endure official mistakes and popular delusions. To him the flag of his country was verily the symbol of her greatness. In its defence he unhesitatingly turned his back on a lucrative and congenial position in civil life, and from a loyal citizen he became a loyal soldier. "I will maintain my allegiance to the Constitution as long as a fragment of it remains," were the short, sharp, decisive words in which he made known his resolution. When the contest was over, no persuasion could induce him to accept political preferment, even the highest in the land. On retiring from his position as General of the Army, he chose rather to return to private life, without a single badge of distinction, save the priceless services he had rendered his country.

Such was SHERMAN, true type of all that is best in our manhood, shining example of the ideal citizen and soldier, to be read and pondered by all men, who, whether under a reign of law or in the throes of revolution, desire to act well their parts. What a glorious life was his to live, what a glorious death, to die in the full assurance, coming from the hearts and consciences of the people, that he had nobly

performed his duty, that he had deserved well of the Republic.

Very respectfully yours,

(Signed,)   THOS. HILLHOUSE.

To the Secretary of the Chamber of Commerce,
New-York.

The preamble and resolutions were unanimously adopted.

A Committee, consisting of the President of the Chamber, ALEXANDER E. ORR, WILLIAM E. DODGE, ABRAM S. HEWITT, J. EDWARD SIMMONS, SAMUEL D. BABCOCK, JOHN H. INMAN, MORRIS K. JESUP, RICHARD T. WILSON and WILLIAM H. WEBB was appointed to attend the funeral of General SHERMAN.

CHARLES S. SMITH,

President.

GEORGE WILSON,
    Secretary.

NEW-YORK, *February* 17, 1891.

www.ingramcontent.com/pod-product-compliance
Lightning Source LLC
Chambersburg PA
CBHW022157020726
47496CB00008B/2762